CW00556772

Grammy's Goodbye Window

Written by Beverly Van Alstyne Krol

Illustrated by Michele Schweitzer

Paperback ISBN: 978-1-64719-643-1
Hardcover ISBN: 978-1-64719-644-8

Dedicated to my Mommy, who was
the best Grammy ever,

And to my darling grandchildren,
who are all blessings to me!

When Grammy comes to visit,
everyone has fun!

They talk, they share lots of stories,
they play games and sing songs...

...lots and lots of songs!

Grammy has SO much fun, that
it's really hard for her to leave.

Even if she is going to see Charles and
Joseph and Eliza the very next day,
leaving their house always seems
to make her a little glum.

But there is one thing that lifts
her spirits and makes
her smile and lets her heart soar...

...and that is Grammy's special
goodbye window!

When she goes to leave, the children
would race to the window and wildly
wave and blow kisses and sign
"I love you" to her.

Many times, they would also make
funny faces and laugh
and laugh until litle tears ran
down their joyous faces!

The children knew how Grammy loved saying goodbye to them at her special window...

Grammy would look.

Grammy would wait.

Grammy would hope
for those beautiful little
faces to appear in that
window to make those
silly faces and wave
and blow those
tender little kisses.

Were Charles and Joseph and Eliza
getting too old to run to the window?

Did they forget all about it?

Many things change when children grow up.

They get taller.

They get busy with all their schoolwork.

And friends and toys.

Sometimes, they even outgrow little traditions that were so much a part of their time together with Grammy.

One day, when Grammy was visiting, Charles said to her, "You look a little unhappy, Grammy. Are you okay?"

And Grammy smiled at how sweet he was to notice and she answered, "It's almost time to leave and I miss you when I'm not with you, so leaving you always makes me sad."

When the time came, Grammy backed out of the driveway...

...and much to her delight and surprise...

...three beaming, enthusiastic children stood in her goodbye window.

They were waving frantically. They were blowing kisses. And...they were laughing so hard that they had tears running down their joyous faces!

Tears came to Grammy's eyes and she
smiled with a grateful heart...

...as long as there are people
who love you.

CPSIA information can be obtained
at www.ICGtesting.com
Printed in the USA
BVHW021212180821
614690BV00006B/133